Matt's Mitt
and
Fleet-footed Florence

Other Avon Camelot Books by
Marilyn Sachs

THE BEARS' HOUSE
FRAN ELLEN'S HOUSE

Avon Flare Books

ALMOST FIFTEEN
BABY SISTER
FOURTEEN
JUST LIKE A FRIEND

MARILYN SACHS, a long-time baseball fan, has written many popular books for young readers, including *The Bears' House* and *Fran Ellen's House*, which was an ALA Notable Book. She lives in San Francisco, where she roots for the Giants and for their Bay Area rivals, the Oakland Athletics.

Matt's Mitt
and
Fleet-footed Florence

MARILYN SACHS

Illustrated by Charles Robinson

AN AVON  CAMELOT BOOK

Matt's Mitt was first published in 1975 by Doubleday & Company, Inc., with illustrations by Hilary Knight. *Fleet-Footed Florence* was first published in 1981 by Doubleday & Company, Inc., with different illustrations by Charles Robinson.

AVON BOOKS
A division of
The Hearst Corporation
105 Madison Avenue
New York, New York 10016

Text copyright © 1975, 1981 by Marilyn Sachs
Illustrations copyright © 1988 by Charles Robinson
Published by arrangement with E.P. Dutton, a division of
Penguin Books USA Inc.
Library of Congress Catalog Card Number: 88-30980
ISBN: 0-380-70963-5
RL: 3. 2

First Avon Camelot Printing: April 1991

CAMELOT TRADEMARK REG. U.S. PAT. OFF. AND IN OTHER COUNTRIES, MARCA REGISTRADA, HECHO EN U.S.A.

Printed in the U.S.A.

OPM 10 9 8 7 6 5 4 3 2 1

for baseball nuts everywhere,
and especially for my son, Paul

Matt's Mitt

Matt's Mitt

WHEN MATT WAS BORN, HIS parents were very happy. They gave him a party and invited only the best people in the family.

There was his Aunt Louise who came. She was a librarian, and she brought him the *Universe Encyclopedia* as a gift. It had many volumes.

His Uncle Roger, who was an aeronautical engineer, came too. He brought a model of the Wichita Falls Airport, complete with hangars, control towers, airport personnel, airplanes, and one ambulance with flashing lights.

His twin cousins, Bernard and Benedict, were both invited. They were bankers, and they brought a toy bank that was also a music box. If you put a dime in it, a piano played "My Country 'tis of Thee." If you put a quarter in it, two violins and two cellos played the "Star-Spangled Banner," and if you put in fifty cents, a complete orchestra played the first movement of Beethoven's Fifth Symphony. Nothing happened if you put in a penny or a nickel.

There were other important members of the family who came. They gave beautiful and useful presents. Some of them gave cash.

Matt's Uncle William Edgar was not invited, but he came any-

way. Matt's Uncle William Edgar was not an important member of the family. He did not work, and he spent all of his time enjoying himself.

He brought a gift too. It was a baseball mitt. It was blue, and it wasn't new. Matt's mother said thank you because she had good manners. She thought she would throw the mitt away when the party was over and Matt's Uncle William Edgar had gone home.

But she forgot to throw it away. Instead, the mitt was accidentally gathered up with some of the useful and beautiful gifts and put up in the attic until Matt was old enough to appreciate them.

When Matt was seven, he found the mitt. Even though it was large, it fit him perfectly. He kept it with him all the time and slept with it at night.

His mother tried to throw it away while he was sleeping. But Matt's mitt appeared to him in a dream and woke him up in time.

His father offered him a brand-new, expensive mitt with re-inforced air holes and natural rawhide lacing, but Matt said no.

When he started to play base-ball, Matt could hit very well—as

well as other boys. He could run
very well—as well as other boys.
And he could catch very well.
Very, *very* well. Much better than
other boys.

Sometimes a boy on his team
would ask to borrow Matt's mitt.
But the mitt didn't fit on anybody
else's hand. Only on Matt's hand.
On either hand.

Matt grew bigger and bigger.

The mitt stayed the same. But it always fit him.

He was discovered by three baseball scouts when he was seventeen—on the same day.

One asked him to go west and play for the Oakland A's.

One asked him to go east and play for the New York Mets.

And one asked him to go south and play for the Houston Astros.

But he really wanted to go

north and play on the new team that had just been formed—the North Dakota Beavers.

So he said no to the three scouts. The next day he was discovered by a scout from the North Dakota Beavers, and he said yes.

Everybody knows what happened after that. Everybody knows how the North Dakota

Beavers grew up in ten years from a boondoggle team, made up of raw rookies who lost nine games out of ten, to the World Series champions of twelve straight years in a row.

Some say it was because of expert coaching.

Some say it was because of Lefty Katz, the great pitcher.

Others point out how Spike Gomez stole more bases in one year than any two other players together. And some will tell you that Rick Dooley's batting average never fell below .361 in all the years he played for the Beavers.

But most people know it was Matt—and his mitt.

Matt played center field. He could catch jumping—running—

standing—crawling—sitting—
lying—turning—twisting—back-
hand—fronthand—overhand—
underhand—and either hand.

He caught balls that the left
fielder missed and balls that the
right fielder missed.

And he never dropped a ball.
Not once!

But one day he dropped his
mitt on Cookie Rogers's head after Cookie referred to his mitt as
a "mutt." The umpire broke it up
and threw both of them out of the
game for the day.

The umpire's name was Ruth
(Babe) Jackson, the first woman
umpire in the major leagues.
Later, she and Matt got married.
She didn't mind that he kept his
mitt with him all the time.

One day, a jealous outfielder

from a rival team stole Matt's mitt and tried to use it himself. He dyed the mitt brown, but it squeezed his fingers and he could not catch.

Even though it was brown, Matt knew it was his own mitt and rescued it. The jealous outfielder said he only did it for a laugh. But nobody laughed. Not even his own teammates.

Matt scrubbed and scrubbed until he got all the dye off, and his mitt looked like its old blue self again.

The time came when Matt was ready to retire. Matt's mitt was ready to retire too. Its seams were splitting, its blue color was fading to gray, and there were deep wrinkles everywhere.

The last day came. It was in the World Series that the North Dakota Beavers played against the New York Yankees. The score was tied, three games to three. Today would wind it up.

In the bottom of the ninth inning, the score was 2–2, with the Yankees up. The first man walked. The second man doubled.

A man on third and a man on second! And no outs. It looked bad. The manager and the catcher went out to talk to the pitcher. He hung his head. It was all over for the pitcher.

A new pitcher came to the mound. He chewed his gum on the right side of his mouth and threw a curveball with his left hand. The batter swung. Strike one!

The pitcher shifted his gum to the left side of his mouth and threw a sinker with his left hand. The batter did not swing. Strike two!

The pitcher moved his gum back to the right side of his mouth and threw a knuckleball with his left hand. The batter swung.

It looked like a home run. Up, up, up, the ball soared. Above the pitcher's head. Up, up, up. Above the shortstop's head. Up, up, way up, and there were tears in Matt's eyes. He did not want to see his team, the North Dakota Beavers, go down to defeat on his last day.

So he ran back, way back, against the center field wall, and he jumped high and higher and still higher. He was right up under the ball, but it was way above his head. He stretched up his arm as high as it could go, and Beaver fans moaned and screamed because they knew he could not reach it.

They saw the ball zipping its way out over the back wall.

Some say this never happened!

And some say the sun was too bright that day to say for sure what really happened.

But there are those who swear that when Matt could not leap up high enough to reach the ball, Matt's mitt left his hand and made the catch by itself.

When Matt's feet touched the ground again, the mitt was back on his hand, and in the mitt was the ball.

There was silence in the stadium. Even though Matt had caught the ball (or had he?) the runner was advancing from third base on his way home. If only one run scored, the game would be over and the Beavers would lose.

From 461 feet away, Matt could see home plate open and shining in the sun. Nobody had ever thrown a ball so far before. Matt was tired. His arm ached from all that stretching. He took a deep breath. His mitt tightened itself around the ball. He threw, and the ball flew fast, and faster, back over the head of the shortstop, over the head of the pitcher, right smack into the catcher's mitt in plenty of time for the second out, and a throw to third for the third out.

The ballpark exploded. It was a triple play. And Matt was the hero.

The Beavers won the series in the tenth inning.

Later, there were parades, parties, speeches, and medals.

Mostly for Matt.

Five years later, Matt was

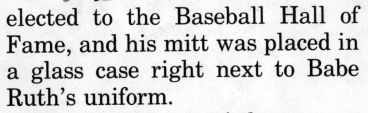

elected to the Baseball Hall of
Fame, and his mitt was placed in
a glass case right next to Babe
Ruth's uniform.

But the mitt wasn't happy.

And Matt wasn't happy.

They missed each other.

So today if you go to the Baseball Hall of Fame in Coopers-
town, New York, you should look
carefully at the guides who show

people around. One of them is a
skinny little fellow with a big
smile.

Watch him carefully. He will
tell you everything you want to
know about Willie Mays's baseball and Joe DiMaggio's bat. He

will stop before each of the famous trophies of great players and tell you facts you never knew.

But see how he passes by the glass case containing a faded blue wrinkled mitt with bursting seams. He does not look at it, and he does not pause or tell you anything about it. The other guides do, but not this one.

But come back in the evening, after the museum has closed and everybody has gone home. Look through the window and watch as the skinny little fellow with the big smile comes back down the hall. Now he stops in front of the case. He unlocks it. He reaches inside, and when he turns around you will see that the faded old blue mitt is on his hand.

Now you know that Matt and his mitt are together again, enjoying the quiet of the evening, hand in hand.

Fleet-footed Florence

Fleet-Footed Florence

MATT, THE FAMOUS BASEBALL hero, had three sons. He hoped that they would become baseball players too.

The first one was named Willie M., after the great hitter. But the only thing Willie M. was great at hitting was his younger brother.

The second one was named Lou B., after the great base stealer. But Lou B. was only great at stealing cookies from the cookie jar.

The third one was named Johnny B., after the great catcher. But the only thing Johnny B. ever caught was colds.

Matt had a daughter too. He didn't expect *her* to become a baseball player, so he named her Florence N., after the great nurse.

One day, there was a fire a few blocks away from where Matt lived. Matt stood on the porch and watched. First, he saw the fire engines go by. Then he saw the police car go by. Then he watched the neighborhood kids run by. He saw Willie M. and Lou B. and Johnny B. then he saw a blue whoosh.

"What," he asked a neighbor, "was that blue whoosh?"

"That blue whoosh," replied the neighbor, "was your daughter, Florence."

Then Matt knew that his daughter, Florence N., would grow up to be a baseball player.

Matt taught her how to hit. And he taught her how to catch. He taught her how to throw. But he did not have to teach her how to run.

When Florence N. grew up, she went to play on her father's old team, the North Dakota Beavers. They had won thirteen World Series in a row in the days Matt played for them. But ever since he left, they had been in a slump.

Florence changed all that. She was the fastest runner in the West. And the fastest runner in the East. The fastest runner in the North. And the fastest runner in the South.

Nobody ever ran as fast as Florence. When she came up to bat, everybody on the opposing team trembled. Because they knew that once she got on base, if there was nobody in front of her, she would come home.

Her fans called her Fleet-Footed Florence, and every game you could hear them shout, *"Hooray for Fleet-Footed Florence!"*

But her enemies called her Flat-Footed Florence or Fat-headed Florence, and often both. Every game, you could hear them shout, *"Phooey on you, Fat-headed, Flat-Footed Florence!"*

Florence played center field. She could run faster than the ball. So when she caught it, if there was a runner trying to advance after the catch, she generally ran in to tag him out.

She specialized in four outs. Whenever the bases were loaded, and she caught a fly ball, she liked to run in and personally tag each player out as he returned to his base.

Sometimes her enemies called, *"Break a leg, Flat-Footed Florence!"*

She did once, tripping over a beer can flung on the field. But she played anyway. And stole two bases instead of three, and put only three men out instead of four.

She could hop faster than most
people could run. Sometimes
when her team was leading, she
would play with one leg tied behind her back.

The North Dakota Beavers won
the pennant the first year Florence came to play on their team.
And that year, they faced their
old enemies, the New York Yankees, in the World Series.

Now, the mightiest Yankee of all
was Fabulous Frankie, the mag-
nificent catcher. Frankie could
catch, and Frankie could hit, and
Frankie could throw.

But Frankie could not run as fast as Florence. And Frankie had a habit of hitting balls out toward center field. Which meant that Florence made more four-outers off Frankie's fly balls than off anybody else's.

This made Frankie angry—very angry, very, *very* angry. So angry, in fact, that he flipped. Every time Florence caught his fly balls or tagged out his teammates, or stole three bases under his nose, he flipped. He flipped so much that he became known as Frankie, the Yankee Flipper.

The worst thing was that he lost his cool. He lost his appetite too, and he lost his sleep. He started letting pitches get by him, and North Dakota Beaver fans

began yelling, *"Fumble-Fingered Frankie, the Yankee Flipper! Yaa! Yaa! Yaa!"*

Nobody called him Fabulous anymore.

One day, after the Beavers had won their third World Series game off the Yankees, and were trying on their fourth, Florence hit a tiny, baby bunt, and came flying around the bases into home plate just as Frankie was picking it up.

They met head on. Eyeball to eyeball. It was the first time they

had ever been so close to one another.

After that, Frankie didn't seem to mind when Florence made four outs off his fly balls. And sometimes, Florence even counted to ten before she ran in and made her four outs.

It was in all the papers: FLEET-FOOTED FLORENCE FLIPS OVER FABULOUS FRANKIE.

Soon after, they got married.

Frankie was traded to the North Dakota Beavers, and he and Florence became the most famous pair of lovers in baseball history. They did live happily ever after, too, but that is not the end of the story.

Florence set so many records that there was no book big

enough to hold them all. Most great baseball players become famous because of their RBI's* or ERA's** or just their BA's.*** Florence, alone, is also famous for being the only player to have an outstanding record of RCI's.****

Of course she had to make sure that each player she carried in touched each base before she did.

One day, an old woman, dressed in a shabby baseball cap and jacket, stood outside the dugout asking for autographs. All the other players hurried by, except for Florence.

*Runs Batted In
**Earned Run Average
***Batting Average
****Runs Carried In

She smiled at the old woman. She inquired after her health. And she autographed her score-card. "Fleet-Footed Florence," said the old woman, "you are the

greatest baseball star who ever lived."

"Ah," sighed Florence, "I wish I might always be a star."

The old woman drew out from under her warm-up jacket a golden baseball. "Because you are good and kind as well as a great star, I have it in my power to grant you your wish."

Then the old woman threw the ball with all her might, and Florence said, "Never fear, ma'am, I will retrieve that ball for you."

So saying, she hurried after the glittering ball. Faster and faster it rolled, and faster and faster Florence ran after it. Out of the stadium, through the parking lot, and over the city streets spun the golden ball. Right behind it came

Florence, laughing in the joy of the race. And right behind Florence came Frankie, crying, "Florence, wait for me!"

Suddenly, the ball rose up into the sky, and Florence reached back for Frankie, and leaped.

Florence was never seen again.

Neither was Frankie. Some say they are raising a family of future ball-players—five girls and four boys.

Some say they are traveling incognito, and can be seen scouting every sandlot where future ballplayers are most likely to be found. Maybe so.

But I think you should look carefully up at the sky on a clear night. Do you really think that flashing, glittering light that moves faster than anything else up there is only a shooting star? Watch! Here it comes again, and see, it really is not a shooting star. You know who it really is racing across the heavens, carrying Frankie in her arms, flying faster than the moon, faster than the sun, faster than any of the other stars.

Fleet-Footed Florence, for all time now, the fastest star in the firmament.

EXTRA! EXTRA!
Read All About It in...

THE
TREEHOUSE
TIMES

(#8) THE GREAT RIP-OFF
75902-0 ($2.95 US/$3.50 Can)

(#7) RATS! 75901-2 ($2.95 US/$3.50 Can)

(#6) THE PRESS MESS
75900-4 ($2.95 US/$3.50 Can)

(#5) DAPHNE TAKES CHARGE
75899-7 ($2.95 US/$3.50 Can)

(#4) FIRST COURSE: TROUBLE
75783-4 ($2.50 US/$2.95 Can)

(#3) SPAGHETTI BREATH
75782-6 ($2.50 US/$2.95 Can)

(#2) THE KICKBALL CRISIS
75781-8 ($2.50 US/$2.95 Can)

(#1) UNDER 12 NOT ALLOWED
75780-X ($2.50 US/$2.95 Can)

Avon Camelot Presents Fantabulous Fun from Mike Thaler, America's "Riddle King"

FRANKENSTEIN'S PANTYHOSE
75613-7 $2.50 US/$2.95 Can

CREAM OF CREATURE FROM THE SCHOOL CAFETERIA
89862-4 $2.50 US/$3.25 Can

A HIPPOPOTAMUS ATE THE TEACHER
78048-8 $2.50 US/$3.50 Can

KING KONG'S UNDERWEAR
89823-3 $2.50 US/$2.95 Can

THERE'S A HIPPOPOTAMUS UNDER MY BED
40238-6 $2.50 US/$3.50 Can

UPSIDE DOWN DAY
89999-X $2.50 US/$2.95 Can

JOIN IN THE FUN AND ADVENTURE WITH

BY **NATALIE STANDIFORD**

SPACE DOG AND ROY   75953-5/$2.95 US/$3.50 Can
When a spaceship crashes in his backyard, Roy gets what he's always wanted—a dog of his very own. But Space Dog is no ordinary pet, he's an explorer from the planet Queekrg on a secret mission to study Earth.

SPACE DOG AND THE PET SHOW 75954-3/$2.95 US/$3.50 Can
Roy wants the whole world to know that Space Dog is special. Space Dog can walk, talk and count, and Roy thinks winning a ribbon at the pet show is a sure thing.

SPACE DOG IN TROUBLE   75955-1/$2.95 US/$3.50 Can
While trying to escape the disgusting, slobbery Blanche, Space Dog runs smack into the dog catcher and ends up spending a night in the pound.

SPACE DOG THE HERO   75956-X/$2.95 US/$3.50 Can
After a burglary in the neighborhood, Roy's dad insists that Space Dog guard the house. Space Dog can do a lot of things—like talk and spell—but scaring away robbers isn't one of them.